This book is due for return on or before the last date shown below.

1 6 OCT 2008

1 7 OCT 2008

2 0 OCT 2008

2 8 OCT 2008

2 0 APR 2009

2 7 NOV 2009

2 3 JUL 2010

2 6 APR 2011

0 8 MAY 2012

0 4 SEP 2012

2 7 SEP 2012

0 2 SEP 2013

1 4 FEB 2014

0 5 NOV 2015

2 0 OCT 2014

3 0 NOV 2015

2 4 APR 2017

RISING

'The truth is inside us.
It is the only place where it can hide.'

nasen

NASEN House, 4/5 Amber Business Village, Amber Close,
Amington, Tamworth, Staffordshire B77 4RP

Rising Stars UK Ltd.
22 Grafton Street, London W1S 4EX
www.risingstars-uk.com

Text © Rising Stars UK Ltd.
The right of Paul Blum to be identified as the author of this work has
been asserted by him in accordance with the Copyright, Design and
Patents Act 1988.

Published 2007
Reprinted 2008

Cover design: Button plc
Illustrator: Aleksandar Sotiroski
Text design and typesetting: pentacor**big**
Publisher: Gill Budgell
Project management and editorial: Lesley Densham
Editor: Maoliosa Kelly
Editorial consultant: Lorraine Petersen

British Library Cataloguing in Publication Data.
A CIP record for this book is available from the British Library.

ISBN: 978 1 84680 181 5

Printed by Craft Print International Limited, Singapore

CHAPTER ONE

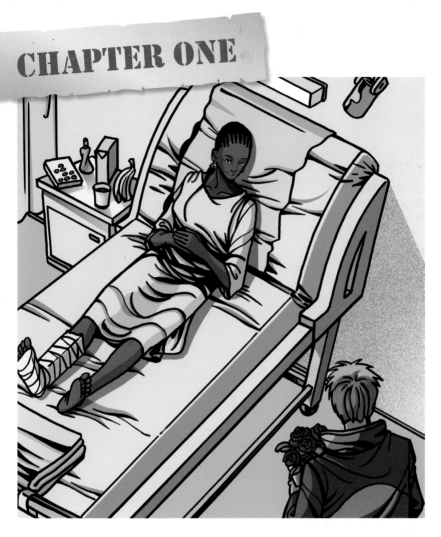

Agent Robert Parker and Agent Laura Turnbull were British Secret Service Agents. They worked for MI5.

Agent Turnbull had broken her foot. She was in hospital. Parker had come to visit her.

"Thanks for the flowers. They're lovely," she said.

He nodded, happy that Turnbull was pleased with him.

"Thanks for the perfume and the chocolates," said Turnbull. Then she whispered, "and the bottle of champagne. I will hide it under the bed where Sister can't see it."

"So how is your leg?"

"It's painful. I feel such a fool."

"It wasn't your fault," he said.

"I got him with a brilliant scissor kick. Then I go and trip over his doorstep, after I arrested him, and break my foot!"

"That's life in this job," he replied. He was beginning to feel nervous.

"Are you OK Parker? You look a bit strange."

Parker looked around the ward before whispering, "Turnbull, I need to speak to you. Can I pull the curtains round your bed?"

"If you want to. What are you going to tell me?" she asked.

Parker whispered, "Commander Watson wants you to go undercover."

"Undercover? I am under cover."
She pointed at the sheet on her bed.

"He wants you to go undercover in this hospital," he said.

"What are you talking about?" she asked.

"Your doctor..." he said.

"Yes, Dr Kripps?" she cut in.

"Well, he loses patients."

"What does that mean?" she asked.

"Three of his patients have come in for operations and disappeared."

"Thanks a lot. That makes me feel good," she replied.

"We have orders to find out what is going on."

"If what you say is true, I might end up dead in my bed," she said.

"Don't get all worked up Turnbull. I know a lot about Doctor Kripps. He has a hobby. He likes to freeze people. He is a world leader on freezing."

"Freezing?" she said, raising her eyebrows.

"Freezing will be big business in the future," he said.

"What's the point of being frozen?" she asked.

"Rich people hope that they can be defrosted when the doctors have found cures for the illness that killed them," Parker told her.

"I am not having that Doctor Kripps anywhere near me. I don't want to die and I don't want to be turned into a block of ice. Why don't *you* pretend you've got a bad back and go undercover?" Turnbull snapped.

"Because I am not a young, attractive woman like you. Three women have disappeared. Take a look at these photos." He passed them to her.

"What is your point?" she said, looking at the pictures.

"They all look a bit like you."

"No they don't," she said. "This one's got big ears. This one has a long nose. This one has red hair."

Parker did not give up. "But they are all females between 25 and 35 with brown eyes and slim figures."

"Just cut it out Parker," she replied.

"I think Dr Kripps is freezing living people. To be exact, young women like you."

"Why would he do that?" she asked.

"To find out things from the living that he can use for the dead. To find out what freezing does to the body."

"It all sounds very creepy," Turnbull said. "Just leave me out of it."

Parker smiled. "The commander didn't think you would be that keen so he said to tell you something."

"What?" she demanded.

"You know Rob Smith? The criminal you caught when you fell over the step?"

"Yeah, the one who tried to kill you with a sword."

"Well, Smith says you beat him up before you arrested him. He says you broke your foot, stamping on his face."

"But Parker that's rubbish. You know ..."

Parker shook his head. "I wasn't there. I was in the car, remember."

"So it's my word against his."

"Don't forget the customer is always right," Parker said.

"But Smith is a mad murderer."

"You know that, I know that. But our boss could use it against you."

"So he is still angry with us about the Atlanta Case," said Turnbull.

"And the baby Werewolf Case," Parker said.

She sighed and shook her head. "So I must do it. Or else we will never get back into his good books again."

It was then that Dr Kripps pulled back the screen.

"Hello, Agent Turnbull. How are you feeling today?" he said, rubbing his hands and smiling.

"My foot is very stiff," she replied.

"Nothing to worry about. We can sort that out in no time. Just a little freezing."

14

Turnbull looked frightened. "Can't I just take some pills?" she asked.

"No. We have got to operate. You will need a plaster on your foot for six weeks."

"Six weeks!"

"Yes, six weeks of complete rest."

The doctor looked at Parker. "Are you a friend?"

"I am her partner."

"Her husband?"

Parker's face went red. "Work partner," he said.

"Well you must look after her. She will need lots of rest."

Turnbull groaned.

When Dr Kripps had gone, Turnbull said, "No way is he freezing me."

"Our time is running out. We need to get on with this case quickly," Parker said, looking at his watch.

"By doing what?" she asked.

"We will go to the mortuary first."

"Not me."

"I'll put a sheet over your head. Wheel you down on a trolley and pretend you are dead."

"Oh no you won't."

"Come on, Turnbull."

"I am not playing a dead body."

"I need a reason to go there," he said.

"Pretending to be dead in this hospital is asking for trouble," she replied.

"Turnbull, we must get back into the commander's good books. Remember what you just said?"

She was silent and sulky. She pulled the sheets right up to the top of her neck. "OK, OK, but don't lock me in a drawer down there by mistake," she said.

Parker found a trolley and hid behind it. He waited until ten o'clock at night. Then Turnbull got out of her bed. She got onto the trolley and he covered her up with a sheet.

"How do I look?" she said.

"You look very dead."

"Now push it carefully. I don't want to get bumped about, Parker."

"Stop talking. There are people about."

CHAPTER TWO

They went down in the lift. Even though it was late at night, a young nurse was waiting there with a tray of medicines. She started to talk to Parker.

"What happened to that one?" she asked.

"Car crash. Hit and run," Parker replied. "Not a pretty sight!"

The lift stopped in the basement.

"This is where I get off," Parker said.

"Me too," replied the nurse.

"Where are you going?" he asked.

"I am dropping these pills off and then picking up pillowcases. Maybe we will see each other later."

"Yeah — sure," Parker muttered.

"Which ward do you work in?" she asked.

Parker froze. He couldn't think of the name of any of the wards.

"North Ward," said a deep voice from the trolley.

Parker nearly jumped out of his skin. The nurse gave him a funny look but she didn't say anything.

MORTUARY

HOSPITAL STAFF ONLY

21

"I'll pop up to North Ward and see you later," she said.

He nodded.

"My name is Jane Brown. What's yours?" she said.

"Robert," he answered.

He was sure he heard somebody laugh. He coughed loudly to cover it up.

"I'll see you then," he said. He pushed the trolley off as quickly as he could.

"Robert," Nurse Brown shouted after him. "You are going the wrong way."

"Oh sorry," he said. "It's my first time down here with a body."

"I'll take you," she said. She put her hand on his shoulder and led him down the corridor.

"See you later, Robert."

"Yeah, bye Jane."

He pushed the trolley through the door and wiped sweat from his face. What a close one!

"You fool! You nearly blew it!" he said to Turnbull.

"I was only helping you out. Fancy not remembering the name of my ward."

"But shouting it out like that when you are supposed to be dead..."

"It got you off the hook Agent Parker. Or should I say Robert?"

"Shut up, Turnbull. I could not believe it when you laughed," he replied.

"You let her chat you up like that, over my dead body."

"No, I didn't," he said angrily.

Turnbull was still laughing when she got off the trolley.

They tiptoed into the mortuary. It was very cold and dark. There were big drawers like filing cabinets everywhere.

"At least it is nice and quiet here," she joked.

"We haven't got long. We must hurry. They may miss you," he whispered.

"What do you want me to do exactly?"

"Keep lookout. I will check this place out."

"Be quick, Parker. It's freezing in here."

He worked fast. Pulling out drawers, shining torches on faces and checking the doctor's records.

"This is fascinating," he called back to her.

"Only you could find this fascinating Parker," she replied. She shone her torch onto the long lines of drawers and shivered.

"Come and see this one, Turnbull," he said.
"Look at the photo."

"Who is it?" she asked.

He shone the torch on the
face.

"The one with the big
ears," she said, as she
took a quick look.

"Yes," he said.

"Not even you could say that she looks like me now,"
said Turnbull. "She's grey!"

Turnbull shivered.

"But is she dead or frozen alive? I can't work it out,"
he said.

Suddenly they heard a door slam and voices coming
nearer.

"Oh no – Parker what shall we do?"

He looked round quickly. "Get on the trolley."

He covered her up quickly.

"And what will you do?" she whispered.

"Get on next to you," he replied.

Before she could say anything he was lying next to her with his arm round her waist.

"Squeeze up, Turnbull," he whispered.

"Get your hands off me," she hissed.

They heard footsteps come into the room. Somebody was opening the drawers.

"Thank you for coming. I know this won't be easy for you. Can you tell me, is this your son?" said a doctor.

"I am going to sneeze," Turnbull whispered.

"Don't be silly."

"I can't help it."

She sneezed and the sheet flew off their heads.
They had no choice but to run for it.

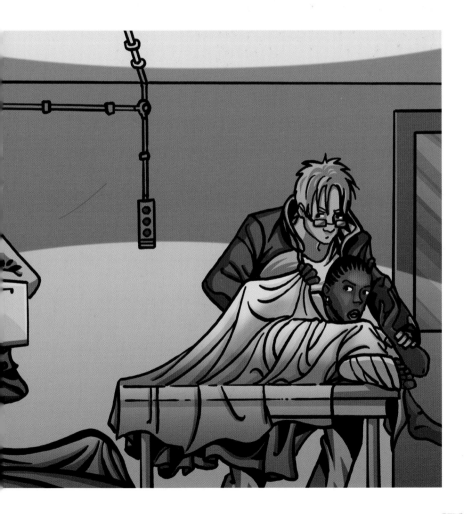

Parker pulled Turnbull along the corridor.

"Slow down Parker. Don't forget my foot is broken," she cried.

He grabbed a trolley and lifted her onto it.
"Let's get you back to your bed before the security guards find us," he said.

"What will you do?" she asked.

"I'll see you in the morning."

CHAPTER THREE

Turnbull was in bed. No one seemed to know that she had been gone. The ward was quiet and peaceful. She fell asleep just as a top secret meeting began.

Dr Kripps, Commander Watson and Nurse Jane were meeting in the office at the end of Turnbull's ward. As they talked, it became clear that Nurse Jane was an MI5 agent.

"Are you sure it was Agent Parker?" asked Kripps.

"Yes," she said.

"Let's check the cameras," Commander Watson said.

They looked at the film of Parker lifting Turnbull onto a trolley.

"They have been in the mortuary," said Kripps.

"They know too much," the commander muttered.

"I must do the operation now," said Kripps. "Come on Agent Brown, we must drug the patient."

Turnbull woke up for a few seconds as a nurse put a needle into her arm. Dr Kripps was at her bedside. He had a big smile on his face. "Nothing to worry about, Laura. We are taking you down to theatre a little earlier than we thought."

"But ..."

"Don't worry. We will fix that foot as good as new."

Turnbull knew something was wrong. She tried to shout out, "Parker, Parker. Help me!"

But no sound came out as the drug started to work. Dr Kripps put her on a trolley and she fell into a deep sleep.

They wheeled her down the corridor quickly. It was five in the morning and dawn was breaking. The birds were singing as they worked on her. They wanted to be finished before the hospital woke up. First, they spent five minutes on her foot and then they spent an hour on her head. Commander Watson watched everything with a quiet smile on his face. He liked it when things went to plan.

When she woke up, Parker was at her bedside with a big bunch of flowers.

"I have had the operation," she said.

"How are you feeling?" he asked.

"I have a headache," she replied.

"Well, I have good news for you," he smiled. "Dr Kripps has been arrested for the murder of three women."

"Who told you?" she asked.

"I rang Commander Watson this morning. He was really pleased with our work last night. It gave him the proof he needed."

"That's funny," said Turnbull. "I am sure I saw Doctor Kripps before my operation."

"Well he was arrested soon after you were back in bed. Somebody called Doctor Brown did your operation."

"I must have been dreaming," said Turnbull, feeling the bump on her head.

CHAPTER FOUR

Three weeks later, Parker and Turnbull went back to the hospital. Turnbull was there to have an X-ray on her foot. Parker was very worried about her. Since her operation she kept forgetting things all the time.

Turnbull went into the X-ray room. The doctor took an X-ray of her foot. Parker had planned what he was going to do. He ran to the window and banged on it.

"Doctor, doctor, a man has fallen over. Can you go and help?" he shouted.

The doctor ran out of the room. Parker's trick had worked. Parker went into the X-ray room. He took two X-rays of Agent Turnbull's head and put the film in his pocket. He was just leaving when the doctor came back.

"You are not allowed in here!" the doctor shouted.

"Sorry doctor, I was just waiting for you," he said.

Later that evening, Parker was in the MI5 lab.
He did not look at the foot X-ray. He looked carefully
at Turnbull's head X-rays for a very long time. There
was a small metal object in Turnbull's skull.

"An alien implant," he whispered to himself.
"Who put it there and why?"

There was a terrible fear in his eyes.

"Agent Turnbull, Laura, I will need to look out for you now. But I must pretend everything is normal until I find out who our real enemy is!" he said.

Parker disappeared into the night.

GLOSSARY OF TERMS

hit and run to do damage and run away

keen enthusiastic

M15 government department responsible for national security

mortuary place where dead bodies are stored

Secret Service Government Intelligence Department

to be in someone's good books to be liked by someone

to get off the hook to get away with something

undercover on a secret operation

went to plan went as planned

you nearly blew it to put a plan in danger of failure

QUIZ

1 Why was Agent Turnbull in hospital?

2 What presents did Agent Parker give her in hospital?

3 What did Commander Watson want Turnbull to do?

4 Who is a world leader on freezing?

5 What happened to three of Dr Kripps' patients?

6 Where did Parker and Turnbull go in the middle of the night?

7 Who did they meet on the way?

8 Who was in the operating theatre with Agent Turnbull?

9 What happened to Agent Turnbull during the operation?

10 What did Agent Parker discover on the X-ray of Turnbull's head?

ABOUT THE AUTHOR

Paul Blum has taught for over twenty years in London inner-city schools.

I wrote The Extraordinary Files for my pupils so they've been tested by some fierce critics (you!). That's why I know you'll enjoy reading them.

I've made the stories edgy in terms of character and content and I've written them using the kind of fast-paced dialogue you'll recognise from television soaps. I hope you'll find The Extraordinary Files an interesting and easy-to-read collection of stories.

ANSWERS TO QUIZ

1 She had broken her foot

2 Flowers, chocolates, perfume and champagne

3 To go undercover in the hospital

4 Dr Kripps

5 They disappeared

6 To the mortuary

7 Nurse Jane

8 Dr Kripps, Nurse Jane and Commander Watson

9 They operated on her foot and also on her head

10 An alien implant